The Tidings
of the Trees

The Tidings
of the Trees

Wolfgang Hilbig
Translated by Isabel Fargo Cole

TWO LINES
PRESS

Originally published as *Die Weiber*, *Alte Abdeckerei*, *Die Kunde von den Bäumen* by Wolfgang Hilbig, Werke, Erzählungen © 2010, S. Fischer Verlag GmbH, Frankfurt am Main

Translation © 2018 by Isabel Fargo Cole

Two Lines Press
582 Market Street, Suite 700, San Francisco, CA 94104
www.twolinespress.com

ISBN 978-1-931883-72-6

Library of Congress Control Number: 2017958708

Cover design by Liliana Lambriev
Cover photo by plainpicture/Folio Images/Peter Gerdehag
Typeset by Jessica Sevey

Printed in the United States of America

1 3 5 7 9 10 8 6 4 2

This project is supported in part by an award from the National Endowment for the Arts.

ART WORKS.
arts.gov

The translation of this work was supported by a grant from the Goethe-Institut, which is funded by the German Ministry of Foreign Affairs.

GOETHE
INSTITUT

Other titles by Wolfgang Hilbig available
from Two Lines Press

Old Rendering Plant
The Sleep of the Righteous

It's increasingly rare to meet
people who can tell a proper story.

— WALTER BENJAMIN

What do I know now, said Waller, of the perplexities that came over me as I tried to write my first stories? Right here I falter: back then I'd never have dared to put it that way! That act of story-writing consisted in an ongoing routine of crossing out words that had found their way to paper with no effort on my part. I seemed to have set them down in some kind of madness—I found whole lines, whole passages filled with words that could have arisen in no other way, all I could accept was the branching framework of the conjunctions—and suddenly it was as though someone, not I, had shone a lamp on them: my words, if I could still read them at all, were the falsest conceivable way to express what I actually wanted to name.

For that matter, I feel I've mentioned these phenomena quite often enough by now—or maybe it

just seems that way, since I've longed to join the le-
gions of writers who think these phenomena worth
mentioning—and I've described them often enough,
defining them now as a failure of my imagination,
now as the inability to think abstractly, perhaps, too,
as the loss of the reality behind the images: I always
meant the same thing, grappling ad nauseam with
this pseudo-problem. Yet my preoccupation has
done nothing to assure me that I may feel myself
to be a writer, sadly not! But lacking actual stories,
as often as I could I've let this plight stand in for
the missing material. Now the whole thing has so
exhausted me that in all seriousness I'd need a new
biography in order to wriggle out from the rough
drafts of my non-authorship. For these drafts have
become the only ground on which I can still move.
Indeed, I am undermined by groundlessness…in-
deed, these drafts besiege me like an impenetrable
barrier, perhaps imaginary, but encroaching upon
me in an unbroken ring: all I can really do is wait
until it strangles me.

Or is it that I feel I'm about to be sliced apart?
Over my narrow circle there's a pendulum, sinking

lower with each swing, hurtling through the air with a hiss that sounds like: Speak!… Speak! — Or it's a saw drawing near, rending the atmosphere with a noise that sounds like: Write!… Write!

And I turn circles in my impenetrable, self-created thicket and cry: Out of here! — Trapped in the creations of my self-prophylaxis, I tell myself: Outside is another life! Perhaps a life just waiting to begin. Perhaps even with a different name to offer me. How much easier to extract stories from a different life… how should I explain my own? What should I make of this life, this life moving to and fro, back and forth, up and down the stairs, the streets, the edges, always on the run…life on the move: I've made it! In my small sphere, crossed by paths paved with precautions…as if letting me trample my misgivings underfoot…here I'm always on my way, always as if my neck were broken: Oh, how I've envied the lives of those who could spend life sitting down. A place to sit, a place to sit! I'd lament, circling my empty chair. When I walked past windows and saw others behind their lit panes—bent over their writing, I imagined, since I took even newspapers for pieces of writing—I believed they must be happy.

And they were, too, or at least they were at peace with their unhappiness! If that was what I wished, I thought, I must never put myself in the awkward position of starting a story with the travails of storytelling. What could be duller, I thought, or more presumptuous, than books about writing books! It might be acceptable, or unavoidable, for tools to produce tools, machines to produce new machines. But when storytelling reconstructs—or, in my case, manufactures—the problems of telling stories, it's the pinnacle of self-circumscription. To me it seems a total submission to inefficacy…I don't know. Literature like that is unworthy of interest.

And yet I must come back to the pendulum. It sounds as though I've described an old paradigm: that telling a story staves off an execution. As long as you can tell stories, you'll go on living, says this paradigm…the executioner, fingering the release handle for the guillotine blade, wants to hear the conclusion of the story first. But this conclusion is not the end, it points toward a new story: another reprieve! Or the Good Lord, grasping the lever of the steam whistle at whose blast the heavenly hosts will speed earthward to bathe their swords in blood, waits for John to finish scribbling his book. These fantasies are all well and good, but the fear of that God and executioner is foreign to me. What drives me is the fear of forgetting the stories. I don't feel threatened, it's the stories that are threatened: I see a darkness preparing to fall upon them. Write…write, I say to myself, or everything will whirl into forgetfulness. Write so the thread won't be severed…a thousand stories are too few. So the flow won't be broken, so the lamps over the desks won't go out. Write, or you'll be without a past, without a future, nothing but a will-less plaything of bureaucracy. You'll lie stored in their databases, retrievable, a calculation, an accounting factor, just part of a sum whose loss was factored in from the beginning… you'll be cannon fodder.

Indeed, I always had the sense of walking on used-up matter, on burned-out material, on cinders, on ash, on slag. Forgetfulness covered the earth and smothered the life that still stirred within it—*if* it still stirred—ceaseless waves of oblivion slid layer by layer over the ground: the dead present was digested and voided until it was nothing but history. Yes, I was walking on the true substance of history: dry, sandy material, forever lifeless, that whirled here and there with the fickleness of all the winds and settled gray or ruddy on all that lay within its diffuse motion's sphere…Waller paused for a moment, seeming to ruminate, then suddenly uttered a bleat of laughter.

What put me on that train of thought, you ask? It only seems to be a digression; I suddenly recalled that I actually did buy a writing desk. The desk, a battered and unsightly thing, was carted past my window one day on the street down which the east wind whistled into town—the wind that bore the worst heat in summer—carrying in the salty, ruddy dust that would later cover that desk's top. The dust was very visible, because the top was black. The desk was being taken to the ash fields, not far away; on an impulse I ran down and paid ten marks for the thing, an above-average sum, more symbolic than anything, but in return the man helped me carry it up the stairs. Up in my apartment, with the help of some bricks, I tried to stabilize the piece of furniture in a horizontal position, which barely succeeded, but now I actually did have a desk.

Weeks and months followed in which the desk tormented me with the demand to be used as such: it was a place from which no one chased me away, whereas the kitchen table had had precisely that agreeable property. Now I sat at the desk and waited for summer, behind me the damp cell of my poorly ventilated, barely heatable room, before me the fog-smeared window; there I hunched, bundled in cardigans and heavy tracksuits, in the baffled shunting of tenacious nights and half-awake days…and when summer came at last and I could open the window a crack, corrosive dust swiftly covered the desktop, settled in my eyes with every move, crunched between my teeth, and clung in the corners of my mouth. It was brought by the hot continental air, and that air carried the distorted and arrhythmic clamor of bells; and the ash had a dry, sour taste I took to be the taste of death. The dust dimmed my empty pages' whiteness on the desk; the one sentence I'd completed in that half year threatened to vanish beneath the ash…then I saw that most of my scraps of paper already bore that sentence, and I was holding the pen, about to set down the same sentence amid the grains of dust again; how long had I paused over the thought that no next sentence would flow from my pen tip? For half a year now I'd been frozen in this clichéd situation! I realized I'd spent days pondering the hunched figure I pre-sented to the public: a figure bent out of shape from sitting on my chairs, bent with the strain of squeez-ing a thought from my head…wobbling on top, the thought in that head, askew between the shoulders, as though I'd been able to approach this obstructive desk only by twists and turns, half attacking, half evading…and these torsions seemed to drill my chair obliquely into a swamp beneath me. Again a spume of ash pelted through the window, the vapors of the night overwhelmed the desk like a disabled boat, a boat in heavy seas, slipping down an endless groundswell, and I could see it only in my contor-tions…no wonder I was a squinting monstrosity by the time I finally fled my desk.

I had no place to sit…the blankness of my

pages always had the same preposterous reasons. Meanwhile I searched for different explanations…I tried to picture a future reader for my output so as to take my cues from him. My themes were utterly foreign to him, indeed the whole environment I conjured up before his eyes could only seem abstruse and outlandish, as though I sought to transport him to a world that, though familiar to him from earlier times, now seemed thrust to the margins, so that no previously valid form of description could be used for it…I wrote for an utterly impossible reader, for one reader alone, and that reader was myself.

The citizens who peopled my streets—if it was even streets I was trying to describe—were dead, vacant figures, or reflections mysteriously left behind in the glass of the shop windows after the original images had long since moved on, and underneath these specters' cold faces was a void; the buildings that lined my streets were mere façades behind which the gray drizzle of a broken film streamed; and at some point the streets themselves broke off for no reason… It was impossible to forget that I was writing about things I'd already lost sight of. — I'm writing about things that are vanishing, I told myself, but whenever I set out to do so, I produce nothing but declarations of that loss…I fail to snatch those vanished things back into the light. If I try to picture a tree, for instance, it's as though I've never seen a tree in my life…it doesn't seem possible to describe a tree, sadly not! If I want to put a tree to paper, I'll have to devise a story in which a tree crops up quite naturally, I said to myself.

And I rushed outside to memorize a tree…for all time, if I can, I want to have it present, for at least one of all the stories that remain to be told, for a tree-lined lane down which I want to wander darkly someday, in one paragraph at least amid the maze of writing may the word *tree* one day resound! — Yet dusk was falling, and my eyes, which were weary and which I didn't trust, could no longer make out the precise…the true nature of a tree. As always on such evenings, I recalled a road outside town that my childhood friends and I had often taken to a village several miles away, trying—a chief pleasure of those early years—to outdo each other by inventing improbable and fantastic tales. At some point we seemed to notice that the realm of the garbage dumps, which covered a vast expanse outside town, had encroached threateningly upon the road. From then on we avoided it, for the evil smells of the garbage heaps, often in clouds of smoke, constantly drifted in a broad front across the road. — Haunted by the mania that in the hours left until morning I must set down a tree in writing, I raced through the commencing night: cherry trees had lined that road, but clearly they were there no longer! For years I'd taken no notice: at some point the trees had vanished from our minds, but there must have been a time when we took their existence for granted. We called that road the *cherry lane*…it was that childhood time when a name so plain and clear was still possible. What ingenuity we've lost since then…if we walked down that road now, even if those cherry trees still lined it, we wouldn't be able to think of the name for it.

It's striking, said Waller, that I just used the word *we*. One might ask, quite rightly, what caused me to do so. — For a moment he broke off and seemed to turn inward.

Of course...he continued at last. In my childhood and youth I did have certain companions to
share my experiences with...it's strange how quickly
I lost sight of them, how they vanished without a
trace. It seems they vanished even before the country closed its borders; but that might be a story for
another time. — Now, using this *we*, I feel it's they,
the vanished, who could add something to my image
of the trees...and cast a shadow into my vanished
image of the trees. — In the vast expanses behind
town that I've referred to as the *garbage dumps*, I always sensed I might stumble across memories of my
former friends. Across some sign of them, or across
their actual forms... Nonsense, all I could find there
now were their ghosts. Surely that was one reason
why I frequented the area...every time I came from
the fields behind the apprenticeship workshop—a
factory where we'd spent three years of our youth
learning some so-called trade—and set foot on the
road we called the cherry lane, an unpleasant feeling
came over me. When I crossed the road I felt awkward, and when I entered the smoke-dark district
whose ground consisted chiefly of heaped-up ash, I

felt I was being followed and observed: once—the thought embarrassed me—I'd perched in one of the cherry trees to perform an escape the others had pulled off more easily. They had simply vanished across the western border into the other part of the country. I seemed to have been impeded in that step by the mysterious attraction the garbage dumps held for me. — Sometimes, after darkness descended on the area, I expected to be addressed at any moment by a familiar, youthful voice coming faintly out of thin air…from sheer nervousness, or to linger for a moment, I'd urinate at the wayside; scanning the darkness before me, a cherry stump behind me, I'd piss a meticulous semicircle in the ashes at my feet. Crossing this line and looking back as I walked onward, I'd think I saw foggy vapors rise from the place I'd circled with my water, and those vapors took on almost human form, those figures' spectral silhouettes beckoned, and words came, barely audible: Don't forget us! — They couldn't follow me; their souls were bound; I'd nailed them to the imaginary cross of a nonexistent cherry tree.

It was during my apprenticeship that I noticed

how the garbage kept encroaching on the cherry lane…a useless road in any case, connecting the town with a village vacated some time ago. Everyone had always known that the village stood atop the coal; now the strip mines had advanced to the front yards, and the hamlet's demolition had been decreed. I recalled the peal of bells ringing from the village steeple; over the years the chiming had grown fainter and fainter, and in the end the notes sounded wrecked by the time they'd crossed the woods to the cherry lane. The invasion of garbage escalated, the rubbish began to encircle the whole forest, advance guards of dead material set out to carve the woods into separate plots, and one of the incursions of garbage came down the cherry lane: following the depletion of the strip mine that would take the village's place, the cherry lane would serve as one of the roads for transporting refuse, the mass of which soon called for a new waste heap. — And the air over the expanses of garbage seemed to grow more and more impermeable; the chimes from the church in the village of W. perished in the burning fumes above the ash and fell to earth like poisoned birds.

Now that I'd remembered the road with the cherry trees, I set out for the area nearly every evening. I began going in pursuit of my memories: even in earlier days the perpetual flight from town had been a sort of ritual for me; as I walked those paths I underwent a visible transformation, the whole thing soon becoming an evening exercise in disappearance. At a certain moment that always recurred at the same spot, I sensed that the distance between the town and myself had grown nearly insurmountable, and I knew I could return to the streets between the houses only at the cost of extreme exhaustion. This moment always came when dusk fell, when the town expired behind me in the afterglow, when the walls and roofs collapsed to a jumble of black crags; and just before everything vanished, a lone water tower loomed from the heap like a strange fungus...or a black fist. Then the sky above me spread wide and seemed to swing up to the east and the north...I seemed to have passed the horizon, with nothing before me now but the plain where the low ruins of sheds or garden shacks cowered, followed by steppes of dry brush from which smoke dispersed in weary eddies, and the woods beyond the cherry lane surged into the night. — Suddenly I'd lost all recollection of town; I was cut off in a way that couldn't be described in terms of the short distance I had covered. This stretch of road, I told myself, could only really be measured in timescales. It's not a matter of a mile or two, it's that I'm ten years…twenty years distant, and over the decades the memory of who I was in that town has escaped me. Returning to town—usually not until dawn—to see a few hunched figures already hurrying to work, I found myself at last in the real world of ghosts; and here I lost hold of the reasons for fleeing town in the evening. — My search for the trees had become a roaming that sufficed in itself…it sufficed to stumble across memories; what I sought was the moment when the things around me sternly recalled how I might have faced them twenty years ago… It seemed that even then I'd had no reply to give them.

For twenty years I'd told myself the same thing: There's no ground beneath my feet! There's no place for me, I said over and over, and I sensed how confused these phrases were, running through my head... There's no place for me to sit, I answered myself, as though recalling a question as to the aim of my roamings, a question I'd asked myself twenty years before.

Each evening I met up with myself on the bleak fields of refuse, each evening I had a rendezvous with my past...in the *ash*, as the area was tersely referred to in town: after the war they'd begun to fill in the unproductive strip mines, first with the rubble of the bombed-out town, later with refuse and ash. Truly, here in the ash I am walking on the ground of my memories...

All that is silenced is rooted in this ground, said Waller to himself, I know all about it...but I also know it won't break its silence. And upon this ground I breathe the air of doom...

Doom? It's the stagnation that was sealed here twenty years ago. It's as if the same air has covered this terrain for twenty years now...for twenty years the same ghosts have been seen in the gloaming of this plain...I am one of them. The shadow of past things, the tremble of depleted matter weaves in the burned-smelling air. Here's the flow of what's been voided, what no longer belongs, what's substanceless and mixed, and the ash seems to stir with imperceptible gasping. — Soon I lost all my reluctance and let the effluvia of the refuse infiltrate me, the colors of the refuse; I absorbed the smells shed by oxidation and rot. I felt eviscerated, but suddenly I sensed I was pervaded by all the messages this historic ground transmitted to the air. It was like an ore that suddenly began to fill me. Underlying everything, like the basis of all sensations, was the unassailable, saturated sourness of the ash, which was indescribable, and which I soon ceased to perceive because my own smell could no longer be told from the ash smell. And soon I knew this smell was in the blank papers on my desk as well…it couldn't be captured in words, but it was there in the dust that held the papers in its grasp.

Returning to town in the early morning light, I seemed to recall that chiming bells had woken me. I looked around; the village of W. had lain to the east. Against the blinding sun the trees loomed like a mirage; before the ash that surged on toward the woods their wispy silhouettes rose like smoke released from the ground. — On my way home I encountered so many trees, mingled with their shadows, that even the cheapest words to describe them eluded me… the cherry lane was no longer to be found.

And above me I seemed to hear the pendulum again, now like the clapper of a bell; the chimes, reeling brittle and broken through the heat, sounded like: *Baum!* — The strokes jarred against the hood of daylight under which I hastened, cowering, fearful that someone might see me…the noise was like a hammering on a piece of iron rail hanging from a wire: the garbagemen were giving the signal for their breakfast break. Or perhaps the sounds came from the workshop where I'd once been apprenticed; its grounds began on the far side of the road to W., surrounded by the ruins of coal factories that had loomed from the landscape, unaltered since the air raids…suddenly everyone everywhere seemed to be jangling iron rails and machine parts, the world was finishing the first third of its working day, a day that must have been bliss…but the poetry of this moment escaped me! I fled through the sonic wall of this noise; at home I sank into the stale air behind my desk, helplessly sorting my papers that boasted but a single sentence, fated to have no echo: The cherry lane has vanished.

In the end the cherry trees, untended, had run wild, and barely bore fruit. They lined up like monstrous cripples along the barely discernible road; the asphalt surface had crumbled, now consisting of a winding strip of black debris, with spurs of forest on the right—underbrush working its way onward—and the ash heaps flooding up from the left. The outermost surges of the ash already washed the roots, and several trunks were singed; on the side toward the road the trees still had dark, leathery leaves, while toward the ash their branches were withered and bare. I imagined that the crooked branches were waving at the onrush of the ash; there was something malignant in the shapes of these trees waiting for their doom; in the evening they were like outlandish monsters whose agonized paralysis might break into a frenzy at any time, and in the morning sun I thought I saw them burning, looming over the road like giant torches, the clamor of the bells and the clang of scrap metal rising above their lurid blaze.

Sometimes I'd sit on a sturdy branch of one of these trees, as the high perch gave me a good view across the whole desolate grounds and all the way to town; I could see over the wooded ridges until they sank down toward the village of W....over the treetops I saw the steeple, back when it still stood, sending out the waves of its chiming all around...I had an excellent view across the garbage heaps, and I watched as they grew. This perch in the tree was a place to reflect on myself, on the perpetually shifting connections...the connections between the natural and the unnatural that preoccupied me... and an observation post from which to survey the environs of the stories that rested unwritten within me. My stories were buried in the ground of this swath of land over which I'd taken up my vigil...and the main figure in these stories was I, Waller!

I saw that figure darting down the labyrinthine paths below like an overcautious animal, first amid the fields and the allotment gardens, searching or on the run, seemingly at random, eyes on the ground yet extremely alert...as though threatened, as though to deceive an observer who, disguised as a scarecrow by heavy black rags, huddled motionless in a tree, gazing across fixedly, perching hour after hour in a cherry tree on the edge of the ash…and in loops and ellipses, in confusingly devised spirals, sometimes in a kind of crabwalk, this form moved toward the center of the garbage dumps. — Sometimes the figure vanished completely, plunging into the underbrush and seeming to hunker down for good, a dark heap of rags…but after quite some time I thought I glimpsed it among the crew responsible for occupational safety and order.

From my elevated perch I could watch the garbagemen, toward whom, I grudgingly admitted, I had initially nursed hostile feelings. There was something connecting us…reason enough to keep my distance, for I already had all the so-called intimacy I needed: I had to fend off the solicitude of my kinsfolk and my colleagues, their astonishment, their curiosity, and finally their disapproval, the flip side of their concern for me. Apart from that, though, I could do as I pleased; they clung to their concern merely to make a point of keeping their aversion alive. It was the completely logical outcome of living crammed together in our tiny state…and ultimately I behaved the same way: I spent hours following the garbagemen's activity suspiciously, with inexplicable interest, but also with indistinct fear: everything they did was a mystery to me, and more and more often it seemed to lack all meaning. At first I thought they were looking for clothing: even in the summer heat I saw them swathed in heavy black rags, beneath which their bodies seemed to boil; lobster-red, as if in perpetual rage, their faces blazed forth from the excess of wrappings with which they bolstered and shielded their bodies. Indeed, all those clothes must have come from the garbage on which they lived; and they always wore their whole wardrobe at once, for ownership claims in the ash were ambiguous. Most of the time I could barely make them out, resting like corpulent animals behind hills of junk, squeezed into slim strips of shadow where they barely stood out from the rubbish. They came to life only when a garbage truck crawled up across the wide field. Scarcely had the load poured out onto the plain with a rattle and a roar, scarcely had the empty vehicle begun to trundle off, when they came running from all sides—even before the fountains of ash had settled, and it must have been hot ash, at least in the winter months—to attack the fuming heap with pitchforks and tongs, with shovels and poles; they smoothed it out in a flash, tugging out all the solid objects, which they scrutinized and dragged away. I couldn't tell what in particular they were looking for; evidently they could use everything...once it looked as if they were hoisting a corpse by its arms and legs, carrying it across the field to an isolated spot where they seemed to unclothe it with lightning speed: I told myself I was seeing ghosts that day...other ghosts than I saw in the evening. It would have been no surprise: in the blazing noon heat I perceived reality through the film of sweat that poured ceaselessly from my brow; the world's surface turned into a rippling image in which I saw most things double; and this image dimmed in the vapors my clothes gave off, for I too was shrouded in heavy black wrappings meant to give me the grotesque semblance of a scarecrow.

It was hard to believe they hadn't found me out yet. What went through their minds under the constant scrutiny of that strange bird perched over there in the branches, motionless as a strung-up mummy? — After the cherry trees had been felled, I'd found myself a place to sit in one of the cars that accumulated at the edge of the ash. Some nights I fell asleep in one of the wrecks, compelled to rest, exhausted by the thoughts that drew me to the area over and over again but refused to give an intelligible reason...and even more exhausting was the effort to suppress all thought of the outcry that awaited me in the event of my return to town, and to the factory. People would notice me there...the garbagemen didn't even seem to see me. Woken in the morning by sawing and hammering as they cut up iron pipes or smashed metal apparatuses to pieces of manageable size, I thought it was impossible that they hadn't taken note of me; when I crawled out from the car's upholstered interior and stole away, they seemed to demonstratively ignore me. I decided to give them a sign that they'd be forced to answer.

I thought I could tell that they'd created separate depots: each contained certain materials to put back into circulation, i.e., recycle, such as scrap metal, paper, or empty bottles. Other depots held unsaleable things: these were the property of the garbagemen, and all manner of worthless junk was allotted to these collections. It was redistributed property, so to speak, and on the ash a perpetual struggle appeared to rage over the contents of these clearly demarcated sites. It seemed possible to me that the most vehement battles were waged for the most preposterous things.

Once I had an idea: I dragged a heavy cast-iron part—half of a broken slide rest from a lathe—from one depot to another and wiped away the drag marks. Sitting in a car, I waited for the arrival of the garbagemen, but as dawn broke I fell asleep. I was woken shortly thereafter by a furious howling and jabbering: at the scene of the crime the entire crew of the garbage heaps faced off belligerently, already shoving each other with hooks and poles. Later, after they'd calmed down, the piece of the slide rest lay unclaimed in an open space between the depots, and they gave it a wide berth. Later that morning they spied me up on the branch of my cherry tree and instantly recognized me as the cause of the mischief.

Swinging their tools like spears, they charged me; as I froze in alarm, they stopped some distance away and attempted to parley with me. But I couldn't understand a word of their gurgling verbiage, and that sent them into a fury again. They picked up stones that crashed a moment later into the branches near me; I jumped out of the tree and fled.

That seemed to signal the end of my relations with them. After that they began to saw down the cherry trees along the lane—in rage, I thought, presumably overwhelmed by rage; I saw their turkey-red faces running with sweat as they attacked the trees like madmen. Within just a few days, several trees had vanished from the start of the lane at the edge of town…they lay cut into pieces, wedged together in barricades, reminding me of so-called *chevaux de frise*, between the piles of waste materials. When I approached the area now, I heard the racket of chainsaws and the rattling and clanking of bulldozers. It seemed wider access routes were being laid through the forest to remove the remains of the village of W.; the bucket chain excavators had advanced to the village's edge and were eating away

at its base, where only a few empty houses now huddled. The rubble was driven off into the ash to fill a
relatively small hole on the northeastern edge of the
plain far away from me, where the garbagemen were
kept constantly busy. I skulked around forlornly
on the opposite side and felt my interest in these
grounds fade away.

Perhaps, too, it was the effect of time, said
Waller, imperceptibly passing time…the operative
word being *imperceptibly*. — Once again he paused
for a while; evidently he was having trouble deciding on a time with which to proceed.

Time in a story can be compared to a river…you
keep standing in the same place on the bank, but
you never step into the same water twice. Probably
I was thinking of standing water…the time of my
past reaches beyond my present; even in the future
I'll be stuck deep in this past, or so I believed. We
lived in a country, cut off, walled in, where we *had*
to end up thinking that time had no real relevance
for us. Time was outside, the future was outside…
outside everything rushed to its doom. Meanwhile,
we've always lived in the past. For us the passage of

time existed only on some withered calendar page printed with a lousy humorous rhyme—clearly the People's Paper Factory had hired someone especially to compose those words of wisdom. — For us the past was what had no closure, no beginning and no end...and that, by the way, meant we'd inevitably be accused of lacking the proper psychological distance. One day we'd have to accuse ourselves of that very thing...with horror! — With horror, thought Waller, we'll realize one day that our thoughts have inexplicably found their way to paper all the same. From a certain distance we'll perceive that the closed society of our thoughts on paper, circumscribed by the escape-proof margins of our pages, has been conceived without distance...without time: without present and future...and is nothing but the past. And this past shall be exposed like a disgrace to the eyes of all the world...before a decade has passed, it will be seen that we'd been lying.

We'd been speaking of a past that kept postponing its end. And it was as though this postponement could wrest forth ever-new stories, or perhaps merely variants of one and the same story. And each story might tell of a time ten years ago, or might date back two or three decades; the sentence I set down at the top of the page—twenty years or two days ago—made no difference whatsoever: The trees of the cherry lane have vanished! There can exist, it seems to me, an infinite series of stories telling how this happened…I can fit only a fraction of them beneath that opening sentence. Or perhaps a barely graspable shadow of ash, light as a breath…for the cherry trees to return, I'd have to tell all the stories about them.

I'd have to tell how I searched for them even while they existed in reality…later, long after I knew of their disappearance, I searched for them still. Reality, in nearly every instance, I thought, has been debased to a worthless product of language.

I shall proceed with a time in which I increasingly began to resemble the garbagemen. It was the time in which—with or without their consent; there had never been the slightest discussion between us—I nearly had a place among them; I lived on their terrain and seemed to gradually and imperceptibly assume their peculiarities. Imperceptibly, time had become an abstraction for me, its passage manifested only in the alternation of day and night, lacking any true progression. And perhaps it was in this respect that I most resembled the garbagemen...they didn't even seem to notice the shift in the seasons, as shown by the clothes they never changed. Increasingly, when I looked in the mirror, I discovered their dull acquiescence in my face, and beneath it I sensed the lurking aggression of which I suspected them. A pall of apathy, perhaps a film of fine ash, hid their savage resolve...resolve to do what, I didn't know; there were just a few unpredictable moments when raw fury glowed in the pupils of their perpetually black-rimmed eyes. My attempts to understand them meant that in time I began to think just as they did, or so I believed at least.

I felt happy for a spell when I learned to be silent like them...they had no speech, at least no intelligible speech; they almost always kept their silence, and silence seemed to grow toward them from the ground underfoot. That ground made no noise, just a whisper now and then when the wind carried off the first thin layer of ash…just the skin of the top layer, beneath which was a second layer, and more layers followed, and underneath were whole strata of ash, a hundred yards thick, a hundred yards into the depths. Historical ash…within this ground was the silence of history, and I was right when I said I had no place on this ground. You can have no place in the history you walk across…I said these words with palpable complacency.

When thoughts like these came to me, I plucked up my courage and ventured out in town again. I immediately ran into colleagues, of course, including several who had long regarded me with suspicion. They told me what I already knew: people had been looking for me, had been looking for me everywhere. I shouldn't be surprised if the police were looking for me too by now. Hadn't I gotten the notes in my mailbox…I'd been warned, hadn't I? — Notes? I asked. — They went on in a more conciliatory tone, looking me over from head to foot: They'd known I'd crop up again, I always did after one of my fits… Maybe even the doctors are looking for you by now! So you don't need the money? By now your take-home pay must be half what it used to be! Obviously it's not even enough for a new pair of pants…you look like you've crawled out of a manure pile. — I gave no reply. — If you don't need the money, why don't you come pick up your papers? Oh, that's it, you don't dare to come back to the factory in those clothes. How can you run around in those things in the middle of the summer…? — It's just a bit of ash, I explained, looking down at my trousers, but the gray-white dust had soaked them to the knee. Anyway, it's not the middle of the summer, it's September.

They moved on, jeering: The doctors are looking for you, the doctors, the shrinks are looking for you everywhere! — I couldn't stand it in town any longer. At the factory my colleagues were perfectly all right, the best, most mild-mannered people, but after work they metamorphosed into mistrustful gawkers who stood nattering and ranting on the market square outside the pub, having their beers handed to them through the open window. I'd never even tried to order a drink there. And I thought of how poorly I got along with my relatives at home, too…my relatives: I lived with my grandmother and my mother; fortunately, I was the only man left in the apartment. — I had categorically demanded *a room of my own*; the apartment was much too small, and with this arrangement I cooped them together in one room. Previously I'd sat in the kitchen when trying to write, and slept in the living room, which was perfectly possible, since they switched off the TV no later than 10 p.m. Now I had the back room to myself; it was the smallest room, even smaller once I stacked my books in there and finally moved in my desk. There I slept and wrote…just as unsuccessfully as at the kitchen table, where I'd felt I was constantly in their way, though in reality they were in mine. Sitting there I went through hideous contortions to hide my pages from them…they definitely had no desire to see them, but I always sat so that the light of the overhead lamp fell on the back of my neck, and as I bent forward my head and shoulders cast a shadow on the paper; what was more, I wrote into the hollow of my hand, my left hand's inner curve, which I curled around the scribbling tip of the pen as though to guard a pearl from a thief's gaze…though of course it wasn't pearls I was putting to paper… When I was alone, and straightened up from my huddle, in the few still-legible sentences I made out nothing but confused reflections on the observation I had put at the beginning, that the cherry lane had vanished; and this beginning was repeated on ten, twenty different pages. The text grew dark before my eyes…and finally I thought I could read part of a description of a thunderstorm during which the trees on the cherry lane were destroyed. It was a failed experiment, I'd been confounded by the time frame, finally deciding that the description meant I'd been surprised *twice* by a storm out there on the ash, years apart…the years that lay in between were a vast mass of time of which I remembered nothing.

Who is it that burned all those masses of time? Waller asked himself. How did that come to pass? — I seem to have changed into a silent ghost after shutting myself in my secluded room. There, in the gloom above my wreck of a desk, I've gradually faded away, and for them, my relatives as I called them, I'm a ghost they're reluctant to recall.

I shall proceed with a year when the cherry trees were already felled, said Waller. It was summer, I sat in that room, trying to think back...I stared out so steadily that the images blurred outside the window. In the street the light faded, and as a pale dusk began, the distant noises of the town sank away, and finally every sound from the adjoining rooms, including the TV's unintelligible murmur—I heard it through the wall, sounding rhetorical—petered out as well. — As always, in the evening sky, almost white above the roofs, I thought I saw the shadows of the cherry lane...they appeared when I raised my head, but always disappeared again: perhaps it was just the star-shaped splatters the sweat made on the paper as it dripped from my face; their shapes left reflections on my retina as I tried long and absently to decipher the faded squiggles of ink beneath the dried liquid...how long had those scribbles already been sinking into the dusty papers' ground!

Is it true that they've vanished? I asked myself then. Hadn't I only just seen them again? A week ago perhaps...in a sudden glance out the window, their silhouettes dimmed by the unclean glass, their crooked growth blurred? And from what window was it that I suddenly seemed to see the cherry trees? A few days ago I actually had been inside the garbagemen's shed, watching a storm through the makeshift window in the corrugated iron wall…but hadn't that been years ago, with the cherry trees still standing, torn from the darkness and magically lit by a rapid succession of lightning flashes? A glance at my trousers, tossed onto the bed beside me, confirmed it: I'd been on the ash just a short time ago; the legs were covered with pale gray filth up past the creases of the knee, the fabric was virtually saturated with ash.

How long ago, I asked myself, had I last been in that area? Years must have passed, and the terrain had changed utterly. The ash had grown into an extensive plain, leveled, but in contrast to earlier times impossible to survey: it was covered with dense brush, strange weeds that stood yards tall, and nothing led through that tangle but narrow paths forming a bewildering labyrinth. I had no idea what that jungle of plants consisted of: dry, tough grass, burdock, reeds…things whose yellow flowers caught the eye at a certain time of year, scrubby mugwort, dingy goldenrod, thickets that thrived better on barren ground than in fertile soil...all the ash seemed ravaged by the breath of their acrid toxic-yellow blossoms or umbels; they steadily filled the air with suffocating clouds of dust, pollen, or fine ash that smelled of evaporating vinegar...or those were the insects rising like swathes of smoke from the bushes; myriads of tiny, barely visible insects wafted up when I approached one of those walls of brush; for a time they'd surge rhythmically through the refracted light like a cloudy flaw, a glimmering discoloration of the air, only to sink into another tangle of bushes a few yards away. For a long time I'd been stumbling down the barely foot-wide paths; believing myself hopelessly lost, I was already forging a new path through the weeds...which I could see over only by jumping into the air...a path toward the sunset, toward the west where the town had to lie, when the bushes unexpectedly opened up before me: I was standing in front of the shed used by the garbagemen, who had kept a wide level space clear in the center of the ash. First I ducked back into the thicket to observe the shack, but I was coughing and gasping, hawking bitter yellow dust from my throat...if they were there, they had to have heard me in the evening hush.

The shack opened up like a memory...I realized at once that I knew it from inside as well, that I'd sat in there by the window already, staring out at the cherry lane...when the trees still existed, perhaps even later...and as though to bear out the memory, at that very moment I heard the first, still-distant rumble of a storm approaching above the woods.

Over the years, rust had covered the corrugated iron walls; in places they had rusted through and were patched with pressboard. Several of the wooden posts rammed slantwise into the ground to shore up the walls had given way, but so much scrap and junk was piled up the walls all around the listing build-ing that they seemed quite stable and unassailable. Next to the charred front door, salvaged from the ash, a window with multiple panes in two casements had been fitted into a hole in the wall...it looked as though the patched-together shards of glass had recently been washed: in other words, the shack had only just been abandoned. — And I recalled the shack's single room, where beams supported the roof from inside as well, with nails for hanging up jackets and tools...and I thought of the long hours I'd spent inside, by day or by night, at a little table by the shoddily glazed window that gave me an unobstructed view over to the cherry lane. Like my window in the apartment on the edge of town, this one opened to the southeast, and caught the light of the rising morning sun...in the afternoon I saw the shadow of the shed's wall stretch across the ash field; into this shadow the glass through which I gazed inscribed its strange reflections, and in this rectangular spot of light I saw a shadow of my own form: I had switched on the lamp that hung behind my head.

To my astonishment, the garbagemen left me in peace; perhaps they'd agreed among themselves to tolerate this strange intruder in their shack...perhaps, I speculated after a time, they had all ended up here just as I had, had come in quite a similar way to the occupation they pursued here. They were leading a life tossed aside from the bustle of the town... they were (to use the technical term) recycling that life on the ash.

Still, I always began by reassuring myself that they'd abandoned the place; first I circled the shack to make sure all was quiet, and on the side opposite the entrance I was usually in for a scare. Again and again I thought I was faced with a heap of corpses piled up by the wall of the shed, the ash field's thickets already encroaching upon them. Of course they were just naked mannequins, I'd seen them before... in the dusk I seemed to see that only male individuals were gathered there. It was an astounding assemblage; apparently the expressions on their faces had fallen out of fashion, they'd been tossed away as refuse, but the garbagemen dug them up again and stacked them behind the shed in a strange and grisly monument. The bottommost dummies had long since gone the way of all flesh: nothing but puddles of liquefied plaster interspersed with filth and ash, metal skeletons sticking through, a mush into which the next layer of dummies settled; they lay on the west side of the shack, where the rain quickly made them one with the ground.

The door and window were on the southeast side, and it was there that I sat at the table, sensing the sophisticated image of transience behind my back, contemplating the decay of all forms: the ash, whose expanse had brought forth an undreamed-of abundance of worthless weeds, was a splendid place for such thoughts.

See how fiction has lost all its charms! I'd think, filled with melancholy. And all pleasure in meaningful games is gone…so it seems, now that I do nothing except hunker in their shack, devoted to my writing…should anyone not believe it, they need only to watch me devoting myself! — It occurred to me that the taciturn relationship between the garbagemen and myself had begun with strange, reciprocally staged tableaux. Once a sort of gatekeeper was set up to meet me at the entrance to their shed: a naked mannequin, leaning on a stick that might have been a sword, its face adorned with terrifying Indian war paint. I stood a second figure beside it, putting a pen in its right hand; I turned the head of the first dummy toward the second one, washing the paint from its face, so that it looked as though the two were in communication. The day after that they turned my figure, the second dummy, and leaned its forehead against the wall, taking the pen from its fingers and inserting it between the buttocks of the slightly spread legs, where it stuck out two thirds of the way, rather obscenely; the other dummy's face gazed into the distance again, one arm raised and outstretched: the gatekeeper gestured out past the grounds, pointing alarmingly eastward, over the cherry lane, toward the woods and beyond…

Against the wall of the shed I placed a discarded park bench I'd found nearby, and sat my figure on it, first freeing its bottom of the writing utensil; now I surrounded the seated figure with more dummies fetched from the depots, forming a semicircle—almost a barricade facing the man on the bench—standing, sitting, or lying in the dust, and, unable to resist a bit of utter kitsch, I had several of my audience members stand around amicably holding hands.

Then several days passed with no new installment to the dialogue, no alteration made to the arrangement…until my seated figure had a book thrust into its hands, which rested on its lap: it was reading, or reciting to its considerable audience. The book was a battered prewar edition of Dostoevsky's *Demons*. — The gatekeeper remained unaltered, now a warning figure: arm outstretched, he pointed across the forest...and it was as though the chiming of bells had just wafted up from the church in W. But beneath this ringing there was suddenly something like the shrill squeals of a herd of sows plunging into an abyss...it was the creaking and screeching of the bulldozers bearing down on the village of W. On top of all this noise came the rolling thunder of a storm.

What an eerie scene! I thought. — Little by little I came to the conclusion—just as eerie, if not more so—that in this day and age only the garbagemen could bring a poetic thought to fruition. Was it because they spent every day in the immediate proximity of an almost mythical experience? It was to them alone that things still spoke of their decay... in their presence things had at last achieved a state of utter worthlessness: and with that they could be contemplated in their authentic being. The essence

of substance opened up before the garbagemen...
while all the others, the consumers whose place
was back in town, turned away from this essence
in horror. In the garbagemen's presence things had
escaped the constraints of their utility and begun
to tell stories...in our eyes they transcended their
transience.

And so it was too, I said, with the cherry trees:
in the end even they were no longer good for anything. Having grown to the point of stony rigidity,
they stood like meaningless threats at the edge of
the ash, and when plans were made to broaden the
road, they were in the way. Filled with black melancholy I gazed across at the place where they had
been...where they had in store one last unforetold
episode: they loomed as shadows in the sky; from
clouds that had grown darker and darker, several
strangely forked shadow-branches trickled like
skeins of water from above, washed in a smoldering
yellow light.

I'd already switched on the lamp in the shack;
I sat at the little table by the window with several
empty pages spread in front of me. Sometimes I

glanced around the room in surprise: the lamp that gave me light was a so-called trouble lamp, a work light cased in black rubber with its bulb protected by a wire cage, the kind I knew from my factory's assembly department; it dangled on its cord from the ceiling behind my head, powered—along with a small hotplate and two machines, a steel saw and a tiny bench drill—from a wooden board with a row of outlets, a rickety and precarious contraption that left all the electric appliances suffering from defective connections. The board lay on the floor; the power cord for the outlets ran up through the roof and, supported by two or three crooked make-shift pylons, extended in the direction of town: just where the road began, sloughing off the bushes and the filth, there was a brick substation. The shed also contained a metal locker that held a tin of ground coffee, an assortment of dishes, mostly unwashed, bent aluminum utensils, an open packet of sugar cubes, and a deck of cards that had turned nearly black; apart from that, the room contained a few chairs cobbled together with wire and a wicker arm-chair full of holes, in which I sat at the table, and in the corner behind the drill were several mattresses with a pile of dust-caked wool blankets.

Contemplating this interior, I felt like an explorer who had drifted off course...that was something, anyway...in a squalid ship's cabin, a makeshift shelter on an island, or a wilderness...the ground beneath me was unsteady, and the storm was unleashed outside. And I tried to make my notes; the pen hastened across the stinging, salt-like dust, the ink ceased to penetrate these sediments, leaving nothing behind on the page, and the pale paper seemed to sink in the ash upon the table... It's the same dust on the desk in my apartment in town, I wanted to note, the ash that's covering the whole town little by little! — The letters no longer fit together. And soon my papers were completely invisible, the dark gained the upper hand; either I hadn't switched on the lamp yet, or it had gone out again in the storm gusts. The rising shadows rubbed themselves thin on the cracked and patched-together window glass; a new rumbling rolled in from the east, over the forest edge swallowed by dark clouds, as though the steeple in W., bell and all, had plunged into the depths of the strip mines…and suddenly, in the first flashes of lightning, I thought I saw the trees of the cherry lane, their grotesque forms emerging once or twice from the darkness, seemingly on the run, making for the edge of the woods with the haste of storm-chased wanderers. Now the wind began to rattle at the shed's metal walls, a menacing noise; I saw the withered shrubs of the ashen steppe bend in waves, and these waves, as though driven by the lashes of a whip, seemed to circle the shack; it was as though the shed stood in the dead-still center of a churning lake. In the lightning's blueish flare, I saw vast masses of ash raised up in the turbulent air and whirled across the plain; they too seemed to gather toward a center above me, then lunge down on the roof like diffuse black beasts, instantly enveloping me in deepest night. Instinctively I held down my papers on the desktop; the shed metamorphosed into a lurching, madly clattering conveyance flying pilotless over raging waves…but it didn't fly away, the building bore up amid the surge of the ash and the storm. And the storm stayed dry, not a drop of water fell from the sky. Amid deafening noise—rattling metal walls, howling wind, and crashing thunder—I got up to search for the board with the outlets; after jiggling at the connection the lamp flickered pathetically, then burned once again...I huddled in the wicker chair at the table, the world impenetrable beyond the window in whose glass shards the lamplight strayed; at last the raging of the storm settled down to a steady course, and around the shed it grew clearer again.

It seemed the storm would pass without a drop of rain. And now I realized that it had grown hotter and hotter inside the shack, perhaps because the storm found no real release. I felt how I was bathed in sweat...for a moment, to my horror, I'd thought I saw myself in the distance, on the sturdy branch of a cherry tree; now, one hand shielding the windowpane from the light, I strained to see whether a lightning flash would reveal the dark, disheveled form again. The trees of the cherry lane had vanished for good.

Sitting there, thought Waller, he was like an enormous bird, feathers ruffling in the wind, struggling not to be hurled from the branch. The lamp swayed back and forth, and its reflected light kept interfering; I couldn't find the uncanny observer again, though the lightning came thick and fast, immersing the terrain in one continuous blue-white conflagration. But, said Waller, I even thought I saw the rope that held that raptor-like figure upright in the tree…a frayed rope, stretching from the neck of the figure—as motionless as a dummy wrapped in an excess of dark rags—to another branch higher up, and it was impossible to tell whether it was already hanging or still hunkering on its perch… If you tried to describe such an image, thought Waller, the whole thing would be nothing short of absurd.

I had fixed my gaze on my papers again, as though to glean some hint about my memory's true circumstances. The sheets were almost buried by fine strands of dust that recalled the rippling forms of a flat sand beach as the water receded: the wind had forced great quantities of fine ash through the cracks in the ramshackle windows, shrouding everything within the shack. And the ash, I thought, coats all my thoughts as well…the ash has inscribed my papers with its uniform and illegible writing. And I've watched these waves of writing rush back and forth, thought Waller, along the lines of the paper, like thoughts that wrote and instantly erased themselves. And in the lower margins, forgetfulness seemed to toss the fleeting eddy of its signature upon the empty pages.

No, having glimpsed that figure in the branches of those visionary cherry trees, I didn't want to lose sight of its fortunes again...if the word fortune isn't too pretentious. — That figure's fate had begun perhaps twenty years prior, in a summer—no one knew now whether that summer had been hot or cold... in this country they've treated *history* so roughly that nothing is left of reality, not even the simplest things—a summer that would later be called the summer of the Wall. In fact, just a year later nothing could be recalled about that summer, less than nothing, for at once it had begun to fill with an atmospheric fiction. Up until that summer the figure I'm speaking of was hardly someone who stood out from his peers; like nearly all the young men his age, he worked in one of the town's many industrial enterprises. After that summer it was as if he had been possessed by a fiction as well. He seemed to be pursuing a notion that could only have arisen in a very confused mind. And that mind was his own mind! said Waller.

His transformation had begun that very same fall, and in the process his thoughts had grown increasingly confused; his explanation for it all was that his previous life had withered and dropped from the branch of a cherry tree. That sounded metaphorical and sentimental...but at any rate it was better than emulating the behavior of everyone else in town. There they all seemed exclusively engaged—almost to the point of doing themselves violence—with ignoring a certain date in that summer, getting on with their lives as before despite that date. In the end they succeeded, living on in the old way without recalling the summer that had barely passed, but they could do so only at the cost of forgetting not just that summer date, but also their life prior to that summer. They actually pulled it off, successfully forgetting all of their previous life along with that date in August...so of course they didn't know whether they really were living as before; but because they didn't know, it didn't matter.

The garbagemen, Waller said to himself, are the only ones who never forgot anything! They couldn't forget, for their job was the constant processing of the material of the past.

No one, I said, could know more about the past, no one could be deeper in the know than the gar-bagemen. But no one asked them, for in the eyes of the world they were the ones with the least say. And if asked, they'd probably have seen themselves the same way; perhaps they ultimately acquiesced in their somnambulistic doings on the terrain of the ash… In actuality, they might think, it's we, out here, who seal and perfect the process of forgetfulness the townspeople struggle with. Yet we ourselves can never forget…and that is the punchline of the story.

Had I approached them because I sensed that they possessed the memories? — No, I said, that's another idea I hit on only later. Another sleight of hand, imposing retroactive meaning on the story. It was much simpler than that: in reality it was that a storm loomed that day, and sitting on the branch of a tree on the cherry lane, I suddenly feared a downpour would start any minute: so I removed the noose from my neck and climbed down from the tree to seek shelter.

That day I'd blundered into the midst of the raging ash that whirled up in tornadoes. Black mountains of dust were raised up beneath the sky and set in scudding motion; at once my face was covered with an ashen crust; blinded and nearly suffocated I stumbled through the surging, whipped-up bushes that by now were barely visible. Reeling from one erupting geyser of filth to the next, my lungs already filled with ash, in utter darkness I collided with the garbagemen's shed. At the last moment I found the door and, with no other choice, escaped inside: that was how I first set foot in their domicile.

I could breathe again; as fits of coughing racked me, the paroxysms outside reached their climax. It was as though the ground's entire top layer were being stripped off and flung at my window; at any moment I feared I'd see the entire shack fly away from over me. Everything outside was in motion: torn-up bushes, flurries of paper and cardboard, even whole panels of sheet metal cartwheeled, booming across the plain. Several times I thought I saw human forms running through the storm outside the window, tumbling, rising up again and fleeing onward; they crashed against the wall of the shack, but sought no refuge inside…later I decided it had been the mannequins, which had been blown over and whirled into disarray. Yet they were lucky enough to remain intact, for the dark cloud fronts moved on without releasing their deluge on the ash.

They were the first things I thought of after the storm, having observed them for days beforehand: those strange naked figures kept cropping up in whole groups. I saw rows of them leaning inertly against the wall of the shed, or lying in a rough circle somewhere in the ash, apparently taking a sunbath; as a rule they lay clustered, almost wedged together—not even obscenely so, rigid as they were—somewhere amid the bushes, facing their doom. Many of them had been scrapped for trifling defects; if they were missing a hand or a foot it was enough to make them seem dispensable in town. More than once I'd tried to establish contact with them…their flesh-brown visages gave no response, they persisted in the forbidding pride of their striking profiles, clearly turned toward the future… sometimes their faces had been twisted backward, making their poses still more grotesque: stiff arms reared up from these ensembles of figures; broken fingers—still graceful, echoing the gestures of ballet school—pointed off into the distance, usually into the sky, where darkness was gathering, where a menacing clangor came from the air: bells' brittle swan song, a storm's thunder waves.

Then…having blundered for the second time into a dry storm on the ash and sought shelter a second time in the garbagemen's shack…then I seemed to see my former comrades' faces outside the window. For a moment we gazed coldly into each other's eyes…they did so more than I, for my lids were crusted with dust, nearly clogged, grainy ash grinding away at my pupils, and the caustic salt drawing out my ceaseless tears. I wondered if I'd really recognized their dead faces; the storm had already chased them away… Don't forget us! I thought I heard them cry, waving wildly from the shadowy vortices before immediately vanishing again. — Another time, during the first storm—I told myself—it was tears of rage and shame that flooded down my crusted cheeks. In secret I looked back on this as though on some romantic scene...until the thought came that it must have been they who'd thwarted me back then, at least they'd played a part in it. And they'd thwarted me so thoroughly that twenty years had passed like no time at all, and I'd lost the ability to sort separate episodes in my memory into their true time frames. Their plea was unnecessary: they had slipped my mind, but I had not forgotten them. What should I call them? My colleagues, my acquaintances, my housemates, my countrymen, my neighbors...the custodians of literature who'd gathered me to their dead bosoms, my friends, the literati who'd invented me...the citizens, the natives, the indigenous people, the members of society outside and inside the shop windows, all those who were a part of it, my *secret societies* that swaddled me and stripped me again and pointed to the grease on my skin...all the ones I'd wanted to write about, to write as though they were within me: the ones who had thwarted my stories.

That was it—they were the population of my stories! They were The People, and I didn't believe that they could ever change.

Suddenly I had to shake my head at the nonsense I'd let myself believe. Had I wanted to write about those characters, the ones who strolled through the center of town in the afternoon, reflected in the shop windows? About those citizens put on display by the State's clothing industry? About those role models from whose chiseled masks the axioms of the State stared out? For a long time I'd actually thought I could do it. But again and again I'd found that despite all my efforts I never managed to pull off a perfectly normal character: characters like the perfectly normal people I seemed to encounter all day long at the apprenticeship workshop, at my workplace, on the streets of town, in the house where I lived…they resisted my attempts to put them to paper, just as I was resisted by a perfectly normal tree glimpsed at the side of the road. Normality was normal because it had lost its stories…only when the mask of normality was torn off did reasons for stories exist once again. I had seen it in myself: as long as I fit seamlessly into the preplanned routine of the workshop, and later the routine of the factory after moving on from the workshop, there were no stories for me. Only once I was on the run, once I'd vanished in search of my stories, and stopped showing up at the factory...and had been absent for two weeks, or more...only then did the material of my stories coalesce before me. Suddenly, in fact, it was essential to tell stories, because the time during which I seemed to have gone missing had to be described...if only for my own justification.

Even I was increasingly unclear about where I'd been, and which time I'd been in: so I had to explain myself to myself! It was for myself that I needed a justification...but these would no longer have been stories describing the life of The People I lived among...they were no longer legal stories. They were stories of the refuse, the refusal of this People! They were cast-aside stories, found only in the troubling places outside town.

I could tell myself these things, but I had yet to prove them. And my excuse was that every morning, as soon as the sun rose, I fled back into town...into

that urban terrain, foreign to me, clearly quite un-
familiar: all at once the town had become a place of
secrets. Suddenly, the ideas of the stories seemed to
be hiding here…while their material, their substance
might be out there in the open country, their moti-
vation had been forgotten in town. So I was always
wavering: the long stagnant days in town drove me
out of my room and to the garbage heaps. But there
the night was as long as the day that had passed:
there, amid the dark heaps, I found myself surrounded by the true stuff of stagnation.

I have no place to sit! I told myself, and above
me was the boundless block of the dark…it was like
a gigantic space of soundlessness through which
a sudden soft whistle floated, a tenuous, rhythmically throbbing tone that seemed to draw near, as
I waited to be touched by its motion through the
air. Usually I fell asleep waiting. Drawn up double, virtually crumpled by the weight of the night
like a block of seamlessly stacked years, I'd fall at
last into a deep sleep…waking again perhaps mere
minutes later. All the while my brow had lain in
ashes, in the ashes among the still-empty sheets

on the tiny, precarious table, so rickety that even in my sleep I thought I had to steady it as though it might collapse beneath my head. Now the working day woke, hammering and clanging, and the sun glared through the fractured glass of the panes…by roundabout ways I slunk into town. — Perhaps I'd be able to write there…perhaps there, behind one of the corners I skulked around, would loom the spectral motive suddenly unveiling my theme: that youthful idea I'd lost, suddenly revealed in a familiar face, almost ghostly in the early light toward which I'd return after a long circuit through various streets I no longer seemed to know…and I'd stare into the pale visage of a memory, avert my eyes, then quicken my pace.

Up in my room I pondered these things for hours: paralysis quickly caught up with me—this paralysis was quicker than I—and in vain I gazed after the light that vanished with the morning, and my memory subsided into weariness. I knew all too well that the majority of the People I belonged to lived in conformity…what a gloomy thought; of course, they had no choice. It would have been a miracle if any of my former friends had been exceptions. They too—just like the ninety-eight-percent majority—kept to the scope appropriate to them, where, except in little things, there was no cause to seek a language that deviated from the one formulated for them by the State, by language's custodians. A keen instinct told the members of the majority—and there was no need to keep warning them—that deviant language would have pitted them against the State's axioms; they sensed it from long historical experience, passed down to them without their conscious awareness. — These same axioms stared down at me from the walls of the trade school, from banners proclaiming things like: *We Strive to Emulate the Best among Us! For Outstanding Learning Outcomes to Strengthen Our Socialist Homeland!* — Though I felt that few of the town's citizens really strived for anything, all of them, almost all, did seem in full agreement, agreeing with the selection of clothing that was promised to them, and feeling strengthened when their prescribed set of paths was described as the *Homeland*. And when plaster, cement, and carbon monoxide rained down on their back yards, they knew progress was at work. They were the majority, and because they were so close to me, I had no thoughts about them. There was no language in me for them—or about them—though they walked toward me on the street each day, though I saw them in the factory and in the halls of bureaucracy and sitting next to me on public transportation...though their idols had been set up in stone and on posters in all of the town's empty spaces, though they were reflected in the town center's shop windows, and when I stood beside them, I watched them greet their comrades behind the glass and make arrangements with them.

At some point I had to admit that I hated them...and this thought made me lose sympathy for myself. Perhaps it had started when I left the workshop and switched to the main factory. Suddenly I'd had to realize that my life's course was predetermined...it was *their* course, the one they demonstrated for me daily: and instantly I had to start hating myself too. A predetermined course? I had to admit that ultimately—if the world I lived in had its way—that course was already set. A completed course: that was what to call my life! — From that day on I never gave another thought to my age.

My existence seemed to have shrunk to an area as long and as wide as the road I was supposed to take to work every day...hitherto I had merely intuited this, as an unrest that I alone seemed to sense! There was a rumor that the country's borders would be closed—soon, in the near future, this very summer...forever? It was a thought you could think only if you didn't count yourself among the ones who'd be affected. I began to seek reflections of the rumor in the faces I encountered; I'd stop next to them and peer covertly at the masks that gazed back from the panes of the shop windows: the citizens' visages made no comment on the rumor, positive or negative. They were afraid! No...I saw no sign of that, there was contentment in their expressions; as always, they'd made their peace with misfortune even before it happened. On their brows I saw no move to escape.

Though the wind had nearly died down, the un-rest continued in front of my window. Outside was a roaming of bodies in gray darkness...or it was de-tached limbs I'd glimpsed, the mannequins, returned from the darkness, crippled vestiges of them scared up once more from their decay…or the vestiges of trees, split-off branches, limbs of trees…they were memory-images from the time that for me had ceased to pass years ago, images that rushed toward me when I shut my eyes, blinded by the lamp that swung through my field of vision…the pendulum of the lamp sliced off layers of thought and exposed new images when it swung back behind my head as a mere glimmer in the windowpane…in which my silhouette could be seen, framed by splintering glints, and the pendulum seemed to swing through my brain…and at last I held the lamp still to steady my reflection in the glass, to make out behind the glass the resurrected mannequins that were neither young nor old…but there was nothing to be seen, nothing but the battle between the images of reality and a few broken-off memories from my mind. It was a juxtaposition of bloated trivialities…the storm, amid one last ponderous effort to catch its breath, had collapsed, and only the remnants of scattered gusts still swept to and fro. I sat where I was in the trembling light; I blew the fine ash from the papers I saw in front of me, as though I might go on writing at any moment, as though that time…the long epoch between the first sentence and a second sentence hadn't existed. — Outside, through the parting clouds, the first spears of light shot down, dying out within seconds only to reappear elsewhere; maybe it had rained somewhere after all, for mists suddenly rose up, rolling close over the ground in lagging waves; from enormous heights ash sank down upon the plain, having been blown so far up that its falling seemed without origin, unearthly; and its cataracts, with moonbeams swimming in the ruddy haze about them, shrouded my view for a long time. Amid the ceaseless downward surging of this uncanny, atomized matter, I'd had an apprehension of how much time had passed me by: since the thunderstorm that first chased me into this shack… decades, I repeat, that I was not aware of; only the recurrence of this dry storm reminded me that I had aged—that I had lived without giving life a thought.

Now I felt that for all these years I'd been shielded by the light beam of the lamp in this shack. And finally, night by night, I'd slumped down farther over this table, cut off from the clamor of the ordinary folks outside this light, which did not even illuminate all the corners within the shed...I was tolerated only by the garbagemen, who did not disturb me in my long idleness, and it seemed agreed that I in turn would not disturb them in their grim industry. And here, perhaps, I'd become a model for them: here, bowed over my endless first sentence... over the pages that have turned yellow now, while I've turned old and gray: gray-red ash has eaten deep into my skin, the salt in the ash has clouded my sight, my ears are clogged with the ash crystals, and my lips have assumed the ash's stone-gray hue. And there's ash all over my clothes, my shoes and socks are full of it...no, I'm buried in it up to the ankles, soon up to the knees, and all my pockets are filled with ash, my earnings from all these years, and all my thoughts are infiltrated by the ghastly substance of the ash, which is nothing but gray stuff, dry and thundery, hard and unfeeling and burned-out. And over the years the fields of ash encircling me have sprawled almost to infinity, nothing calls to mind the motion of time now...oh, throughout those years, faintly smiling, I recalled the concept of time, and it seemed that truck after truck filled with its dead burned substance had been driven to the margins of the inhabited territories. And I felt that those margins had spread and had long since become a massive preponderance, that the ash had long ago gained an irreversible ascendancy over the settlements of life...oh, that amid this immensity, the towns and villages were mere nutshells adrift upon a sea.

Here I was...I'd been here for a near-eternity, and already I was almost a ghost...a monster, shaped from the substance of eternity, a sculpture of ash muffled in ancient ghostly garments...and the garbagemen, who believed in mythical creatures, had long ago accepted me as their ghost, slinking around me breathlessly and on tiptoe; and they'd consigned the citizens from the shop windows to the garbage, for I was the true artwork of their time, I was the statue which alone fulfilled all their time's aesthetic requirements, their time that was no time at all... the trees of the cherry lane have vanished; this single sentence, long since extinguished and grown cold, stood there upon the page, and they'd given me infinite time to write a second one. That first sentence was like the uniform sifting of the ash, it was followed by a relentless flood of thoughts, but nothing was willing to go down on paper…nothing, not since I'd been sitting here lurking, watched over by the garbagemen and with memory flowing through me, memory in which I saw myself progressively transformed into one of them: into a figure of their ore-gray, faceless sort, speechless before eternity; and I saw myself living in the ash, deaf and blind and mythical. I sat here evening after evening and thought of many things, but the motive that had led me here refused to come to me.

I recalled how confined this country had become back then, back in my twentieth year. The rumor had come true at last, and the borders had been sealed off. The confinement oppressed me more and more, though the roads I had to take were still there for me.

Again Waller paused and uttered a laugh: a response, it seemed, to some conclusion in his mind that he did not clearly voice.

Even then it was the sense that I had no place
to sit…an absurd sensation that only grew stronger
once the country had become a closed society. For
me it had almost transformed into a soundproof
room, paralysis setting in wherever I looked: the
leading figures of the movement were statues…that
couldn't fail to have a certain effect. — My daily
route to work now seemed too short and monot-
onous. In the morning hours I wandered through
side streets and alleyways where I hadn't set foot
in years, just to have more time, more space for my
thoughts; hemmed in by the state of the country,
these thoughts were a maelstrom that drew me in
inexorably. Every day I arrived for my shift a few
minutes later, a few quarters of an hour, soon hours
late; my life became fraught with conflict, and all my
boredom was a thing of the past. My relations with
the outside world took on a threatening character;
routinely I had to stay on at the factory in the after-
noons to make up lost hours, and soon, as I couldn't
be integrated into any coordinated production pro-
cesses, I was used only for more loosely scheduled,
incidental jobs; all that prevented my dismissal was

the felicitous labor shortage that afflicted all of the industrial enterprises. Meanwhile, my roundabout ways grew longer and longer; in the morning, anticipating more accusations and admonitions at the factory, I was filled with particular dread and procrastinated still more. I spent hours pacing back and forth along out-of-the-way streets, desperately pondering how I might sneak into the factory unnoticed...I seldom succeeded.

Soon I extended my morning rambles out past the town limits, and it was just a question of time before I ranged so far that I no longer managed to show up for work at all. By evening, unrest had already chased me from the house, and I'd wandered around all night; in the morning, back home, I'd collapsed from exhaustion and fallen asleep. Or I'd already reached the ash fields in the morning and suddenly felt severed from all the grounds for my existence in town. So I'd walked on until evening, walked and already saw myself walking through the night again, a dark bundled-up figure, down the bare track of the former cherry lane, on and on in the wrong direction, as though summoned by the errant chiming of bells in the night, a doleful tone as of cracked metal that barked out over the forest and merged into a sawing and a crunching. — Soon I'd reached the end of the woods, abysses gaped before me, their depths barely touched by the moonlight…the village of W. had stood here, a place I'd never visited while it still existed. It was too late for that, as it was for so many things, time had hurried onward, and I hadn't heeded it; I headed back; I couldn't afford to let my mind stray. — The woods had been chopped into sections, sliced apart by countless aisles for the vehicles that had cleared the land; perhaps that too lay decades in the past; it was too late even for my thoughts or for the words I chose to ward off forgetfulness; and it was as though I'd headed back without doing what I'd come for. I hurried down the moonlit aisles as though to outrun melancholy, and again I had the sense of walking back through the years.

As I stepped out of the forest, the full moon-light behind me now, I saw that the broad vehicle tracks continued out over the ash. They had even broken through the matted, dust-dry weeds: one of these aisles led me straight to the garbagemen's metal shed, which I could see from a great distance. At first I thought the shack was lit from within, but then I realized it was the moon reflected in the windowpanes…from a certain angle, as I came closer, it gave the illusion of a figure, upper body visible in the light of the lamp overhead… The window wasn't far above the ground, so he had to be sitting: and thus I saw that shadow once again, and his posture showed that he was bent over some unseen thing in the glare of the lamp that revealed him to me so blurrily. It wasn't hard to believe I saw him writing…or pausing in the strain of seizing a distant thought, his gaze sunk into the paper on which his hand with the pen poised, trembling. — There was no doubt that I'd seen myself again… I'm the one sitting there by the window: sitting there always, never knowing how I got to this place! Or they really did just seat one of their mannequins at the table! Perhaps to frighten me…or to make up for the loss of my existence? For perhaps one day I really did vanish beyond the woods, where the sky still held the echo of vanished bells, where the abysses gaped. And perhaps in all these twenty years they haven't grown used to the loss. And in this way, as a perfectly replicated effigy of their thoughts, I really have spent twenty years sitting by their window...

Twenty years, filled with thoughts—at least giving that appearance—bending over this table by the window and probably long since thinking the thoughts of the garbagemen, nothing else being possible in this place! For twenty years—or so they saw it—I viewed the world with their eyes, and finally felt the sun with their skin. Twenty years, the breath of the ash on the skin of my brow, and nothing on the plain outside escaped me. — Who was that young man out there—younger than he looked—who shuffled at such a slant through the wind of the ash...? And how he kept glancing around: a hunted man, straining his senses in all directions like an animal...so we set up a dummy to show him the way. Of course it was only as a joke, but he went that way...the next day we turned the dummy around, and he went in the other direction...we turned the figure around again, he followed, and we laughed until the metal of the shack laughed with us. There was just one path he rejected; it was impossible to show him the way back to town. He preferred to spend the night in old wrecked cars on the grounds. Or he slept in the storage shed; we made him a bed of old mattresses, we've got plenty out here in the garbage heaps. Or he'd perch in a tree over there, staring this way...the municipal office had long since instructed us to fell them; the first tree was felled, and the next day he perched in the second tree.

What people that town produces! Nothing but dead, useless things come out of the town and can pass across the borders. Perhaps we used to be something like that...there's no one here but people who never learned to make their fortune in town. And people who prefer misfortune out here to misfortune in town. Out here, it has the advantage that it can't be confused with fortune. Here no one needs to deceive himself. Here no one needs to forget. Each of us remembers the moment when he wanted to snuff himself out. A moment like a bolt from the blue! — I'd always *deceived myself* that I was living... over there in town!

From the town, from the municipal offices, almost nothing reaches us on the grounds, except letters. Directives, for instance—most of them a year out of date. Accounts settled, far too late. Fat envelopes stuffed with cash! Overdue sick pay for people who've been gone for years. Years ago the beneficiary bit the dust. Sometimes the folks in the office remember some jubilee that's rolled around out here, and we're sent an enormous gift basket, topped with spoiled salamis going oozy. But the guest of honor is already a corpse…we might have buried him long ago on the edge of the grounds. Then he gets his basket from the Party; you see, there were people who came out to join us rather than leave the Party, it was simpler that way, and in the end we buried them with all the honors. No one in town seems to know how many of us still exist. They seem to think in terms of four or five men per shift, which means we get money for fifteen to twenty. But even if it were fifty men that emerged at the crack of dawn from their dwellings at the edge of town—a whole swarm of ants setting out into the ash in the dark—they still wouldn't know. In reality there are only three or four of us, but they've long since forgotten that back at the office. When they drive their cars up to the boom gate at the edge of town…they call it an inspection… they peer through the haze and the smoke and see the mannequins at work. These inspectors are used to living with mock-ups of reality…and they pay the dummies quite well, for as we all know, the sanitation department is understaffed. That's not due to a lack of mannequins—far from it, rarely have so many bitten the dust—it's solely because of the increase in garbage. You see: progress reigns in town! Progress is the order of the day in the town's shop windows and all across the land, especially now that the land has been transformed into a closed society…that was a step in a desirable direction, they say, fond of that sort of alliteration. Quite right: progressive times bring a revolution of forgetfulness, and in the process lots of new designs grace the shop windows. And then out here we neutralize what has been forgotten. Yes, all this is executed outside town, past the boom gate, past a warning sign: *Unauthorized Dumping of Household Waste on the Grounds Is Strictly Prohibited.* — *The Town Council.*

We don't concern ourselves with that; to each his own private revolution, we think. At the same time—one hand washes the other—we make sure we pocket no bribes less than ten marks; we let them pay for their forgetfulness. — That's another reason why we never stop thinking about all the forgotten things. There's something in all the junk here on the grounds…in all this property, in all the abandoned secondary wealth, in the old-fashioned cultural artifacts: amid broken coffee mills, radios and toilet seats, rusty bicycles and desks; amid Party congress leaflets and Party personnel files and photo albums and ash; amid the thousands and thousands of tons of the past…in all this there's something that hasn't yet learned to be silent. And we haven't learned silence any more than it has. We're always thinking about what all this junk has to say to us, out here on the grounds. What food for thought it gives us, the junk that the town's digested and thinks is now eliminated. It's as though all these cultural artifacts would rather be with us, we think, grinning. Before that we watched the people sanctify their property. They hung banners on it, celebrated it with fireworks and carillons. They took pictures of it, kept files on it; they gave it new names and showed it on TV and went to bed with it. We simply waited, knowing that all these things come out to the grounds once they've been digested and shat out. We've always been here. We've always waited here and we've always existed: here…we've been here since time out of mind, grinning expectantly, here on the grounds. When they held up the icons of the new gods and hauled them through town—gigantic, twenty times life size, painted on red pasteboard—we watched them. They always turned back at the edge of town, those processions with their pasteboard faces and flags and brass-band music…as a joke we set up our dummies to show them the way. But they turned around at the boom gate; of course they never saw the dummies. Unperturbed, we grinned; impatience is no strength of ours. For one day they'll all end up here, on the grounds: whole generations of pasteboard heads are already buried in the ash beneath us. All those faces that got to be God for a while are buried down below now; we've got a whole grove of the gods down there. Layer upon layer, era after era, and if we thought a bit, we could even say what order they're stacked in, down there in the depths. But why should we think about it? It's enough to think that we've always been up here and are likely to remain. At any rate, we'll never get down very far…we think, never far enough to come close, say, to God Number Ten, between the royal court and the accounting department, we think, because only our thoughts can drill down that deep. We ourselves will always stay up on the surface: as though the world were a garden, we think, the blossoms always bloom on top…

Of course, some of us have already lost our bloom. And one day perhaps we too will be digested—it's quite certain, of course. And even then only a tiny bit of us will be washed down to the bottom; it rarely rains out here over the ash, the storms are short and dry. The greater part of us will whirl through the air as fine dust. And in the summer, when the hot inland breeze blows from the east, we'll infiltrate the town like fine bitter salt; we'll creep through all the window cracks and the new acquisitions in the rooms will be coated with gray, and for the first time these new possessions will be looked at askance. In the summer heat, when the dry storms echo in the atmosphere, we, dust that we are, will be borne up to prodigious heights, flying through the air with the storm, and the thunder will be below us. And we'll hear it like bells…far below, in the abysses below, like the forgotten gods' self-celebration.

And perhaps the trees are down there too, and in a little spell of madness we'll see them again. — Doubtless it's the madness that rises from the empty papers on the trembling table by that dust-blind window that distorts the reflections and granulates the contours, and between the glass striations they seem to rise from the depths once more, streaks of trees, limbs of trees: and so the ash has long since described them! — These are some of the melancholy thoughts that cross our minds out here on the grounds. Yes, they emerge from the glaring light in which we sit motionless, and the dust on the paper seems to increase with them; they are so filled with madness and peculiar, static fantasies that dust is all they can become. — And the trees should long since have been described as ash. Clearly they can't be described in any other way: and thus they remain indescribable. — The thought of the cherry trees is painful as a fissure a nail draws across the glass, diagonally across the glass that cries out: *Described!* And their reality seems crossed out for all time. — Only in the ash to which the trees have reverted has their essence been revealed. And they have always told of this essence, though without any subject…a *sujet*, an idea for a story, those were things the trees disdained. If there were such a thing as a language of the trees—and suddenly I refused to doubt it—it was storytelling without motive, a stream of story that followed only the slow rhythms at work in the place where the trees were…imperceptible to me as I incessantly searched for the sujet for a story. They had spoken without cease—they had spoken to me, but through all these decades I'd never noticed it, because my sujet was the stagnation in this land— the endless flux of ebb and flow in their silence was their speaking: speaking about the eternal twilight of the seasons whose comings and goings surrounded them always, slower still than the revolving of day and night and the converging of the storms. And there was a speech in the trees that always ended in darkness…no, even in darkness it didn't end, it merely spoke more softly than ever, and I recalled the nameless whisper of their leaves in the unseen. It was a language of return, permanently revolving around the existence of those leaves themselves, and thus around the permanence of the Earth itself, and thus it spoke of the universe in which each leaf revolved with the Earth, and in the darkness the leaves went on rippling…like ash, and the swells of the ash went on into the darkness, and never ceased, even when the ash-red gloaming came, inaudibly soft, and the short day with its blue gloaming at dusk, when autumn sank its cool claws into the blue ash, or when the spring loosened the ash again, and on and on when the leaves and the ash required no more words, and the leaves of paper chafed together in the dust, and the dust chafed whisperingly at time that turned in space, on and on with that empty chafing in the dark that passed like years and had no age.

And the years of age had begun to chime, long

and hollow, and there was no more escape. This was what befell me when the country's borders closed; from one day to the next all hope of life was past. And I thought that here I'd found my place to stand now! The life that lay ahead of me was in the stranglehold of borders…and at that moment I knew I couldn't accept even the mildest form of a border. No! — Youth had passed, I could toss it on the refuse heap. I had to hurry; in the greatest of haste I had to make for the place where I'd be old…sick, invalid, senile, a wreck, an inconvenience. I had to be an unserviceable part in this society if I wanted to cross its border. That was the truth, and no explanations, no tricks of philosophy, culture, economics, or social policy could hide the fact: the years of youth had passed. Once I'd staggered around like the embodiment of all human misfortune, like world-weariness personified…now that romantic bluff had been called. It was time to muster all my malice and turn myself into a cripple. And the dialectics of this maneuver seemed to entail looking like an unthinking idiot and stoically going along with everything. This thought, and it alone, had induced me to climb back down from the branch of the last tree left standing on the cherry lane.

For three or four days—in late August of that death-bringing year—I walked through town with a smile on my face, wondering what characteristics I'd have to acquire now, straightaway, after the recent news whose words kept blurring in my brain. — At the factory that Monday an unexpected assembly was convened during the lunch break. A speaker, some man I didn't know, announced the news in an agitated voice, standing on a chair with his left foot planted on the edge of a marking table…between the lines, his flimsy explanations seemed to beg us to sympathize with the measures taken by the Party and the government. His words barely reached me, seeming to boil away far above me in the haze beneath the hall's ceiling. They merely confirmed a situation long anticipated, yet declared impossible; the astonishing thing was that suddenly it was supposed to be reality. For about ten days I went on working, jaded and unmoved, then one afternoon I switched off the machine and left the factory. Outside a few drops of rain had fallen, but quickly dried; for days the rumble of thunder had circled the town, but the atmosphere found no release. Burned-smelling air washed the roofs in continuous waves; the sky seemed to smolder, sometimes appearing almost black. And there was a barking in the distance like artillery salvos. Sweating with haste, I hobbled through the burned-out streets—I'd been absent from work for three days, but that was nothing new—and tried to think what had to be done now. Perhaps I should immediately turn criminal, so as to be expelled from this suffocating space as soon as possible...or become a fascist or something of the sort. Excellent...better still, perhaps, an agent of the secret service. And so my thoughts raced, but nothing struck me as a really certain remedy. Some people, it seemed, had quickly slipped through gaps in the border...I didn't dare try. I had to admit it was too late: I'd missed the last train; I'd slept away my life. There was no place for me in this country, and its borders had been closed. It was late afternoon, and for more than an hour I'd been perched on the branch of the cherry tree; with great care I'd placed the noose around my neck and pulled it tight; I couldn't find an end to my thoughts.

It makes no sense, I thought over and over, it makes no sense to cut a process short like that. If I must give my assessment: the country has turned into a hotbed of misfortune—misfortune and stagnation—and doubtless it will all soon come to a head. So if I go on living under these conditions, precisely by maintaining my existence I'll degenerate in the quickest way possible. Without hope of change there's no prospect of emerging unscathed. Misfortune ages you, I said to myself. The constant simulation of nonsense causes habituation, until even in your own mind it seems perfectly persuasive. That sort of trick requires oppression, and this backwater will breed plenty of it. Will that plenty be enough?… Certainly it will, if only you firmly believe so. And so I can already imagine no worse affliction than continuing to live in this cloaca. What could be a greater affliction?… Only the misfortune of some West German Communist now left out in the cold, outside the Iron Curtain. If I had the option of joining the West German Communist Party, I'd put in my application right now…but to do that,

I'd have to be outside. I have no choice but to eke out the misfortune and stagnation in here…and act as though things might turn bright again someday.

At that I removed the noose from my neck… before abandoning my perch in the tree, I heard the thunder grow louder; it was approaching, and the first storm gusts swept in. They raised banners and strands of dust from the plain like black and gray-red flames; flickering wildly they moved in from all sides, taking my breath away. I fled across the ash field, where darkness was gathering; and the plain was whipped up like a sea above which aimless storm gusts tumbled.

At the table in the shed I had a long mental struggle, disappointed at my cowardice. In the deafening racket of the metal walls, in the mad light of the lamp that swayed above me and played me for a fool, I was so lonely that I felt hot rage rise within me, bringing tears to my eyes. — It was inconceivable to me that I should belong to a people of whom so many were surely faring likewise! said Waller, shaking his head to himself.

For a long time I stared at the shadows that

loomed crazily from the walls, at the spectral reflections in the windowpane that seemed like grotesque faces, sliced by the swinging light of the lamp. As the storm gradually calmed, the howl of shame within me began to quiet down, slowly becoming immaterial. I recalled the purpose of the papers in front of me, which also seemed thrown into turmoil on the little desktop: it was impossible for me to describe the events' full force while they were still at their peak! And twenty years had not been enough for me to reach this insight. — For twenty years I'd refused to make peace with the moment when, helpless and shivering, I'd climbed down from that cherry tree! And in all that time I was unable to set down a second sentence because the first one seemed wrong to me…and for all those years I was unable to write, struck dead by the hissing stroke of that infamous pendulum. And only now did I think I knew the next sentence that was called for.

The shame is over! — That was the sentence. Now I regret that the witnesses of my defeat, the cherry trees, have vanished. And now it's easy to confess that one day I woke up in the ash; and the speechless storm above it is over. The destruction we once perpetrated has passed its height, transformed into a gentle flow that smooths everything out; gradually the black billows chased up into the sky are returning to their place. The objects describe themselves in the sinking of the ash that covers them, in the flattening of their fury, in the shift from hate to melancholy…the days' glow withdraws beneath the evening clouds. Night falls, and all through the long night I wait for the ghosts of the cherry trees to reappear before me. — I stared out at the plain's dark edge, and sometimes white smoke deceived me, branching and then standing still; for some seconds it stood out against the burning-down horizon. — I've seen it before me for hours tonight, my head already resting on the tabletop, emptied, but now, somewhere above me, there's another sentence that's possible. It's the thought that the cherry trees are finally revealing themselves, in their pale feather-light ash, as fleeting as the blossoms of these trees in recollection…in the filmy, barely noticed recollection behind the faces of my former companions: snow-white, soul-white, so ghostly was the trees' blossoming against death. One more time their shadows glowed forth, red before the rising sky, then trickled away into pale nothingness.

It was dark in the shack; I didn't know whether I had these sentences on paper; at some point, I thought, I'd set them word for word on the rustling lines. I still seemed to hear the dust scratching and scraping. I could make out nothing, saw only the bands of dust and ash that had spread across the pages...the thoughts were already swimming in my brain; in the very next moment the sentences might sink away. It turned pitch-black; I got up and jiggled the cord of my lamp; the light began to flicker, and the lamp went on again at last. Quite right, I'd actually turned the light on hours ago...again I took the pen and searched the paper for a place to pick up the thread, but once more the overhead lamp went out. Angrily I kicked the outlet, and the light flared again. At that, blinded in the constant flickering, I thought I saw a tree branch thrust its twigs through a crack in the door and reach for the cord: the connection was broken, the light went out for the third time...for the fourth time! — I've had enough of your stories, I muttered. With my foot I jiggled the plug until I had light again. But the branch— no doubt about it, it was a piece of firewood from the stack outside the door, remnants of the cherry lane—the twig, its end shaped like a hand, came creeping up once more. Through the narrow crack left open between my weary leaden eyelids, I saw the twigs grope for the outlet: it went dark again. The sentences I'd wanted to write were in an obscure corner in the back of my brain; they slipped further and further into the margins. I decided to go to bed at last. — Dozing off on the uneven, dust-covered bedding in the corner, I thought I heard voices outside the shed door, an utterly incomprehensible muttering, a quarreling and scolding; outside, the gray of dawn began, and a muffled ringing and chiming filtered into my dreams. Metal struck metal, as though somewhere out there loosely hung metal rails, a great number of them, were moving in the morning breeze and knocking together.

WOLFGANG HILBIG (1941–2007) was one of the major German writers to emerge in the postwar era. Though raised in East Germany, he proved so troublesome to the authorities that in 1985 he was granted permission to leave to the West. The author of over twenty books, he received virtually all of Germany's major literary prizes, capped by the 2002 Georg Büchner Prize, Germany's highest literary honor.

ISABEL FARGO COLE is a U.S.-born, Berlin-based writer and translator. Her translations include Wolfgang Hilbig's *The Sleep of the Righteous*, *"I,"* and *Old Rendering Plant*. She has been the recipient of a prestigious PEN/Heim Translation Grant, and her novel *Die grüne Grenze* was a finalist for the 2018 Preis der Leipziger Buchmesse.